"Once in a while, we come across stories that enlighten us and make our lives seem a bit more magical. The story of *Lisa & the Seven Magical Tooth Fairies* takes you through a journey of moonbeams, stars and rainbows...and along the way, helps us see and reach all the gifts our universe has to offer each of us. May all your dreams be realized and all your fears become just puffs of memory as you read Margaret's wonderful story of hope, magic and love."

—Lori Cagiao, special education teacher

"How enjoyable! A wonderful mixture of fantasy and reality. A reminder we're all special, no matter how different we seem."

—Terri Meehan, Grandparent of three

"In this busy world, we tend to look at things just as they are. This book inspired and reminded me to look at things how they could be, covered in a blanket of goodness, hopes and dreams."

—Audrey Martin, Mother of two children

"A mystical fairy tale that has an emotional hook, connecting to fantasy and reality for readers young and old."

—Jorja D. Eder-Duban, public & private school teacher for 30 years

"I read this sweet story with delight, noting the very gentle messages of love and acceptance within. The illustrations were charming, bringing this loving world into the physical present."

—Kat G., The Earthseeds Project

"Stunning ... You don't want to stop turning the pages once Margaret opens her door to this wonderful fairy tale."

—Amanda Knight, Mother of two children

The Seven Magical Tooth Fairies

Miramont Castle
Museum

Helping Children
Find their Way

The Seven Magical Tooth Fairies

Lisa and the Seven Magical Tooth Fairies

Margaret H. Johnson
Illustrations by Beverly Hilliard

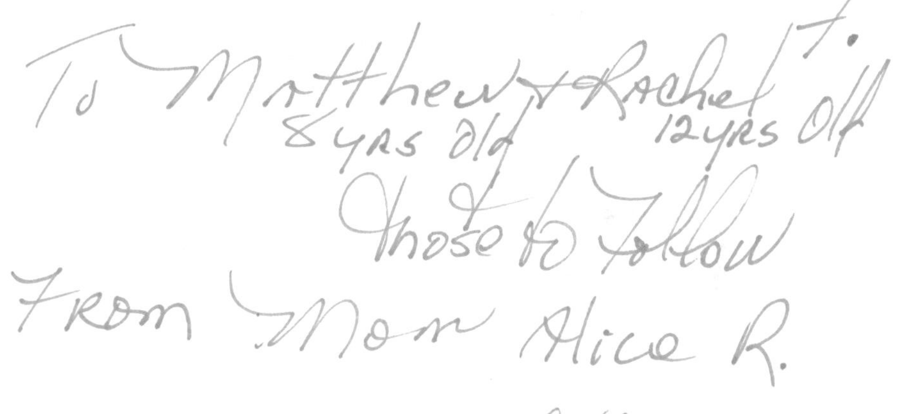

iUniverse, Inc.
New York Lincoln Shanghai

The Seven Magical Tooth Fairies
Lisa and the Seven Magical Tooth Fairies

iUniverse books may be ordered through booksellers or by contacting:

iUniverse
2021 Pine Lake Road, Suite 100
Lincoln, NE 68512
www.iuniverse.com
1-800-Authors (1-800-288-4677)

Written by: Margaret H. Johnson

Illustrations by: Beverly Hilliard

Creative Editor: Theresa Barbera

Editor: S. Heather George

Partial proceeds of this book will be donated on behalf of my readers to non-profit organizations for abused & disabled children.

ISBN-13: 978-0-595-37420-5 (pbk)
ISBN-13: 978-0-595-81813-6 (ebk)
ISBN-10: 0-595-37420-4 (pbk)
ISBN-10: 0-595-81813-7 (ebk)

Printed in the United States of America

The Lights in My Life

Love isn't something you look for.
Love is within you.
Love just is...

My family: Nathan, Quinton, Mason, Maddux & those to follow

Father & Mother: Samuel and Bernarda
Foster Mother: La La

Brothers & Sisters: Arthur, Billy, Manuel,
Michael, Kathy & Bernarda

Special Friends: Dane Barbera & Maggie Knight

Acknowledgments

I thank God for this heavenly book, *The Seven Magical Tooth Fairies* ... I am so fascinated ... I am driven by the King of eternity.

My sincere thanks and deep gratitude to the loving hearts who gave their support and unconditional love in hopes of saving even one child. What an honor it has been to work with them and to be a part of their dedication to this vision in blind faith.

May this book enrich the life of every child who reads it.

Hearts of Gold are: Beverly Hilliard, Theresa Barbera, Heather George, Sterling Jones, Martin Cagiao, Jason Balaam, Dan Rizzo, Steve Knight, Janet Rohan & Warren Epstein

Supported by:
Miramont Castle

Matt Anderson, Mazie Balaam, Louise & Bob Becker, Bob Burr, Carm, Charlie & Lorie Cagiao, Najasila & Janiero Campbell, Theresa Coleman, Malcolm Gill, Johnny Graves, Debbie Tatem Herrera (Australia), Keegan Jenney, Terri Bowmar Jones, Barb Kunkel, Susan LaCava, Vicki & Blake Leiker, Linda Little, Micki Marple, Paula Ann Miller, Jennie & Mallory Morgan, Rebecca Muhl, Derrick Norwood, Clara Robb, Todd Romero, Olatha Sherman, Nancy Smith, Louis Tutt, Curt Volkman, Don & Shirley Wick, Ceira Cavanaugh, Kinsey Knight, Mandy Leiker, Emma Martin

I would also like to thank the Shriners of North America for all they do for the children of this country, Canada, Mexico and the Pacific Rim. These twenty-two hospitals—specializing in Orthopaedic, Burns & Spinal Care—are giving the children of the world a better chance in life.

Special Thanks:

Keller Williams Premier Realty, the company with a heart, is proud to support this book which promotes kindness and caring to children. The amazing spirit of Margaret shines through this heart-warming story that is sure to become a classic.

Rosalinda Chaney
Keller Williams Premier Realty
Team Leader & CEO

Firefighters, not only controllers of the flame,

but friends & guardians of the children ...

~ Dedication ~

For those who believe in...Miracles, Dreams & Wishes...
and for those who want to...

Faith of the Mustard Seed

I
dedicate this
book to all who have
been a part of abuse and survived.
For it is these individuals who dwelled
in the beginning of darkness and survived
because of blind faith. Through their darkness
remained one thought: The Light At The End Of
The Tunnel—their belief that the situation could not
possibly last forever...To the disabled who have
endured the ridicule and cruelty of childhood
and negligence of the world, this book is
written in hope that the world can
one day come to a greater and
gentler understanding of
their struggles.

~ Validation ~

The Seven Magical Tooth Fairies

Queen Melody

Contents

Introduction

When a child loses a baby tooth, it is placed under their pillow. Shortly after, while the child sleeps, a Tooth Fairy comes and takes the tooth, replacing it with money.

Many fables have been written about Tooth Fairies. What do they look like? Where do they come from? Is there more than one? Even with all the stories, not all children have known about the presence of the Seven Magical Tooth Fairies.

Now, these small heavenly creatures reveal themselves and are here to touch the hearts of children everywhere. They want to share a very special message about the magical powers of the heart.

The Tooth Fairies live in a Crystal Castle, in a very special kingdom—a heavenly place unknown to man. Their moon is quarter shaped with seven bright stars all around it. The stars represent the life of each Tooth Fairy. Their sun glows with all the colors of the rainbow. Their days are never hot, and their nights are never cold. Mother Nature provides them with all that they need including Great Magical Powers. The Seven Tooth Fairies are Dawn, Dusk, Crystal, Eden, Garnet, Heart and Queen Melody.

Mother Nature grants each Tooth Fairy one wish in their Eternal Life. However, the Tooth Fairy—Heart—whose wish is granted first, wishes to become mortal. Mother Nature reluctantly grants Heart her wish with the understanding that Heart is to return to the kingdom in seven years or she will remain a mortal forever.

During Heart's journey, she realizes that becoming a mortal is not as glamorous as she thought it was going to be.

In exchange for the knowledge Heart learns as a mortal, she reveals the magical powers of the heart to children everywhere. Hopefully, in the end, this incredible wish may help change the outlook of mankind.

~ A Fairy Tale ~

The Blue Rose

~ Chapter One ~

A Queen is Born

One spring morning, the day the Tooth Fairies had waited for so long had finally arrived. Garnet came flying through the kingdom, announcing at the top of her voice, "Our Queen has arrived! She's here! She's here!"

One of the Tooth Fairies caught up with Garnet and asked, "What Queen?"

"Remember?" Garnet excitedly replied. "Mother Nature promised us a Queen!"

"Oh, yes, I remember now. How do you know our Queen has arrived?" she asked.

Garnet was so excited and out of breath that she could barely talk.

"Well, I couldn't sleep this morning," she said, catching her breath. "So I decided to get up early and go out to the garden.

While I was sitting there, a film of stardust suddenly fell upon one of the roses. It must be her! Hurry! Hurry!"

Upon hearing the long-awaited news, all of the Tooth Fairies flew like the wind into the garden.

Garnet was right. There was the new Queen sleeping on the biggest blue rose in the garden. She appeared as beautiful as anyone could have imagined. The Queen wore a bright green dress, and a full crown of seven multicolored stars floated above her head. She was covered with stardust from head to toe. As she wiggled from side to side, you could see her wavy black hair and two beauty marks on her face. A butterfly gently settled on her shoulder.

The Queen was awakened by the murmuring of the Tooth Fairies as they stood around her. As she opened her emerald green eyes and blinked, dewdrops on her eyelashes caught the rays of the morning sun. She slowly stood up and stretched, and then smiled; for she knew she was exactly where she was supposed to be. She wore a brilliant green gown and shoes that sparkled brightly in the early morning light. She appeared to be a bit larger than the other Tooth Fairies but just as weightless. She was surrounded by five beautiful little creatures with very excited, smiling faces. She immediately felt the warmth of love and kindness all around her.

The Tooth Fairies all had long blond hair, almond-shaped emerald green eyes with long black eyelashes, the prettiest small ruby red lips, and soft pink cheeks. They were no taller than twelve inches in height and their incredibly large wings were as big as their bodies. Each Tooth Fairy had a beauty mark somewhere on her face, and each wore a different brightly-colored gown. They all wore belts with a shining star for a buckle, matching the color of their gowns; and above their heads, floated a matching brilliant colored star.

Suddenly the Queen felt a tingling along her spine. She looked over her shoulder and was amazed to see enchanting wings begin to unfold on her back. They grew and grew until they were larger than her body. Now she truly looked like these lovely little creatures with their butterfly-like wings.

Without warning, a breeze flowed through the garden and a soft and gentle unseen voice spoke to the Queen...

"Welcome, I am Mother Nature, and you have been chosen Queen of the Magical Tooth Fairies. Your name will be Queen Melody. Your destiny is to make believers of nonbelievers by using your magical wisdom with children everywhere. Your wings are magical and give you the power to fly. You have power to hear children talking from wherever they may be. You can become life-size whenever you wish and invisible whenever you choose. You can move things without touching them. You can speak without moving your lips. You also have incredible powers of the heart and mind, which you will discover on your own."

"You, Queen Melody, have been given the gift of music and are blessed with eternal life. The greatest of all the powers you possess is the power of love. Apply it to all you do, think, and say for your power is useless without it. However, there is one thing you must always remember! Be very careful of your wings, for if you injure them in any way, you will lose your magical powers until they mend. You are also granted one wish in your eternal life, so be very careful what you wish for."

"Queen Melody," Mother Nature continued, *"when children lose a tooth to make room for grown-up teeth, they place the tooth under their pillow. During the night while they sleep, you will take the tooth and replace it with money. When you return, you will place the tooth in the garden. Through your dreams, you will know which children to visit."*

"Mother Nature, where do I get the money?" asked Queen Melody.

"The money you need is created from the beautiful shells that you will see in our lake," replied Mother Nature.

"Now, look into the sky and you will see another star appearing

around your moon. I have placed that star to assure you that I am here with you always; and, remember that when you seek me with all your heart, you will find me..."

Then instantly as the voice began, it disappeared.

Now, there were six stars, instead of five, around their quarter moon.

All the Tooth Fairies gathered about Queen Melody to help her down from the blue rose. They immediately formed a circle around her and briefly introduced themselves to her one by one.

The first Fairy stepped forward wearing a radiant yellow gown. "My name is Dawn, your Majesty. My job is to greet the sun every morning." Dawn was very shy, but didn't hesitate to let Queen Melody know by her bright smile that she was thrilled with Queen Melody's presence. She then stepped back into the circle.

Another Tooth Fairy stepped forward wearing the color orange. "My name is Eden, your Majesty. My job is to care for the garden." She was the one Tooth Fairy who loved to giggle, and she bowed and giggled all the way through her introduction with the Queen.

Next, the Tooth Fairy dressed in blue stepped forward. "Your Majesty, my name is Dusk. I greet the evening sky each night."

"That's if she isn't eating, sleeping or racing madly about the kingdom on one of the magical flowers," said one of the Tooth Fairies, and all the other Tooth Fairies giggled shyly.

"You like to eat and sleep, do you?" Queen Melody asked, smiling at Dusk.

"Yes, your Majesty," replied Dusk. When she couldn't be found, her friends knew they could find her eating or sleeping somewhere in the garden.

The Tooth Fairy in pink flew forward and bowed. "My name is Crystal, your Majesty, and I'm in charge of making sure the castle remains in order."

The last Tooth Fairy stepped forward, wearing the color lavender. "My name is Garnet, your Majesty, and I watch over the Tooth

Fairies and help with anything they need, and I will do the same for you."

Queen Melody noticed that none of the Tooth Fairies touched the ground, although they could if they wanted to. She could see that the moment they almost touched the ground, their wings would start to flutter, fold and unfold like a butterfly, bringing them back up.

Then Queen Melody's wings began to flutter, taking her off the rose. Once firmly in the air, the tooth fairies took flight escorting Queen Melody towards the Crystal Castle.

Garnet
announces the arrival of the Queen

~ Chapter Two ~

The Kingdom

The castle was made of crystal and gold, and a rainbow towered over the entire kingdom, causing the castle to radiate with many colors. The path leading to it was made of many clouds, which appeared to look like marshmallows. There was also an invisible force field surrounding it, which only a Tooth Fairy possessed the power to pass through. Upon entering the castle, there were butterflies to greet them.

As they gracefully flew down the hall, they entered Queen Melody's room. She saw the floor was covered with daisies and the bed posts were made of crystal and gold. Her blanket and pillows were made of rose petals.

Queen Melody stood in awe at what she saw and said, "Is this my room?"

"Yes," replied Garnet.

"Are all the rooms in the castle this beautiful?" asked Queen Melody.

"Oh yes," replied Garnet. "However, it has never glowed like this before!"

The butterflies took Queen Melody by surprise as they flew in and out of the room, fluttering all around her so she would notice them. They were landing on her hair and kissing her hands. Queen Melody slowly fluttered around the bed softly petting this flower and that flower, leaning over to smell their exquisite fragrance.

"They smell wonderful!" she said happily. No sooner had she said that—without warning—she was instantly off the ground and floating about the room. Then slowly and gently, she floated back down. The Tooth Fairies could tell by the look on her face that the flowers had taken her totally by surprise, and they all began to giggle.

"Queen Melody, I should have warned you," Garnet said. "The flowers have a fragrance which is a secret scent that will magically lift you into the air."

"Now, what would you like to do next?"

"I would like to use my powers to disappear and reappear in another place in the kingdom," said Queen Melody.

"If you wish," said Garnet.

So, Queen Melody then took Garnet's hand, closed her eyes, and went into deep thought. She remembered the garden with the lake that Mother Nature told her about. In the twinkling of an eye, they were in the garden. She was so excited about what she had done that she giggled in delight and said, "Oh, Garnet—it's so beautiful here."

In the garden, she saw a lake so crystal clear it appeared to look more like a mirror than water. She could see all the way to the bottom and saw the Magical Shells at the bottom of the lake.

There was something magical about this lake—it appeared to be a kingdom all its own with very special fish. Like the Tooth Fairies, the fish were very beautiful and the colors on their bodies glowed brilliantly. The reflection of their multicolored sun seemed to penetrate through the water, creating the brilliance and illumination of their bodies.

Some of the fish could be seen resting while others were scurrying about as though they were playing tag or hide-and-seek. There were plants for them to lie under or hide in and brilliant colored shells which made the water twinkle. The fish could be seen picking them up in their mouths and re-arranging them for some special purpose.

There were flowers floating on the water, which were magical, and the Fairies used them like magic carpets to fly about the kingdom. The Tooth Fairies loved using them to float out to the middle of the lake and would ask the fish to dance and play with them. The fish could surface and playfully walk and dance on the water. They did this by using their tails to move themselves about. Oh, how the Tooth Fairies delighted in them!

The only fish who could actually talk was Star. When the Tooth Fairies needed money for the children's teeth they called on Star. He would swim as close to the surface as possible; as he talked, bubbles would surface above the water, float into the air and burst into words.

'You've called for me?' Star would ask. 'How may I serve you?'

The Tooth Fairies would answer, 'We need some money for the children's teeth, please.'

Star then called on the other fish to gather Magical Shells from the bottom of the lake and bring them to the surface. The Magical Shells then instantly turned into money.

The Tooth Fairies then bowed and said, 'Thank you, kind fish,' as the fish swam away.

On the other side of the lake stood the Happy Willow Trees with their smiling faces; they spoke with very deep voices.

Giti

There were Magical Mushrooms that could walk and talk, and change into any color they wished to be. But the mushroom Giti spent all her time dancing to amuse those in the garden. She was delightful.

The Tooth Fairies, however, were still the most beautiful creatures in the kingdom.

Queen Melody and Garnet gently flew over the lake and sat on the flowers. As they floated about, Queen Melody discovered that she could hum. To her amazement, the flowers, the Happy Willow Trees, and the Magical Mushrooms began to hum with her, creating music in the air. To her further delight, the winds whistled by them, adding more music to which they could dance.

Garnet sat for a moment, captivated by what was going on around her and thought, "What a beautiful Queen we've been granted. She is beautiful, kind and has added music to our kingdom."

Queen Melody stopped humming, looked at Garnet and asked, "Garnet, how did you and the other Tooth Fairies arrive here?"

"The same way you did, your Majesty," replied Garnet. "Mother Nature created this beautiful place for us to live in; then she created us one at a time. I was the first Tooth Fairy. As time went by, more and more children were born into the world and it was getting very difficult for me to visit all of them by myself. So, Mother Nature decided to create more of us; and chose you to be our Queen."

"Now, would you like to try your magical powers again? I know you must be hungry by now. Maybe you can try to bring us something to eat from the garden," Garnet suggested.

"But how?" asked Queen Melody.

"The same way you thought us to the garden," replied Garnet.

So, Queen Melody closed her eyes and went into deep thought, and instantly fruit appeared upon their laps. She was pleased at what she had done and giggled in delight.

"Oh, Garnet," Queen Melody said, "I'm having so much fun!" All of a sudden—right before Garnet's eyes—Queen Melody disappeared off the floating flower.

"Garnet!" called Queen Melody. "I'm up here. Come join me!"

Garnet looked up to see Queen Melody sitting on top of the largest rainbow in the garden and flew up to join her. There together, they ate their fruit.

Queen Melody had come to realize that in this kingdom all that was lovely, good, kind, joyful, and peaceful lived in perfect harmony with each other.

Queen Melody

~ Chapter Three ~

A Missing Fairy

That evening, as Queen Melody slept, she dreamed of a little girl asleep in her bed. When Queen Melody awoke in the morning, she remembered the dream and a bright circle of light that glowed all around this little girl's bed. Little did she know that this child was indeed very, very special. Queen Melody rushed out of bed and flew straight for Garnet's room, and with great excitement, shared her dream with Garnet.

Garnet listened, and then reminded Queen Melody that she would dream about the children she would visit.

"Do you remember when Mother Nature told you how a child will lose a baby tooth and we visit them while they sleep and leave them money?"

"Yes," replied Queen Melody.

"Well, the fish in the lake named Star is the one who lets the other fish know when we need money for the children. And the fish will go to the bottom of the lake and bring us the shells. When they reach the surface, the shells magically turn into coins right there in the fishes' mouths, and those are the coins we take to the children. When we take the tooth that is under their pillow, we replace it with a coin. Then, it's up to us to return the baby tooth to Mother Nature."

"I remember," replied Queen Melody. "But what does Mother Nature do with the tooth?"

"Only Mother Nature knows that," answered Garnet. "When we bring them back, we merely place them in the garden, and they disappear. Queen Melody, you will dream of this little girl again, and in that dream you will know when it's time to take her tooth."

So that very night, just as Garnet had said, Queen Melody dreamed of the little girl once again. And again the bright circle of light appeared around her bed.

Queen Melody saw the little girl rise out of bed very early. It was so early that the sun wasn't even up yet. The little girl went to get a drink of water and then went straight to her parents' bedroom and woke up her mother.

"Mother," she whispered, so as not to wake up her father, "My tooth is loose. I woke up to get a drink of water because I was thirsty. As I was drinking, my tooth wiggled. Mother, that means the Tooth Fairy is going to come for my tooth. I have a friend in school who lost her tooth, and she told me all about the Tooth Fairy."

"All right, honey," her mother whispered back. "Now you go back to bed. It's still terribly early and we'll talk about this later, alright?"

"Okay, Mommy," she said, excitedly and went back to bed. The moment she fell asleep the glowing circle of light again appeared around her bed.

In the morning when Queen Melody awoke, she remembered her dream. The bright circle of light that appeared around the little girl was really puzzling her.

Now wanting Garnet to come to her room, she closed her eyes and thought about Garnet. When she opened her eyes, Garnet appeared.

"Garnet," exclaimed Queen Melody, "I dreamed of the little girl again, and a bright circle of light keeps appearing around her bed. What does the light mean?"

Garnet looked puzzled. "Queen Melody, I have no idea. We must call upon Mother Nature. Maybe she can tell us what this is all about. First, we need to awaken the other Tooth Fairies and tell them about your dream. Then we'll all go to the garden together, form a circle around you and join hands. This will enable us to call on Mother Nature and ask her what the circle of light means."

So, with a mere thought, Garnet brought the Tooth Fairies together. Instantly they appeared, one by one in Queen Melody's room.

"Why are we up so early?" yawned Dusk. "It's not even time for the sun to rise."

Garnet looked at her and said, "There's something we need to do this very moment and we need to do it together in the garden!" Garnet closed her eyes and in silence shared with them Queen Melody's dream and the circle of light around the child's bed. All the Tooth Fairies agreed that this was something very different and none of them had ever experienced this before. So, they agreed to call on Mother Nature.

Then, Garnet opened her eyes, looked at each Tooth Fairy, and off they flew towards the garden. Once there, they formed a circle around Queen Melody, joined hands, and called out repeatedly in their sweet little voices:

> *"Mother Nature, we call on thee*
> *Knowing you will hear our plea.*
> *There's a little girl we do not know*
> *With a circle of light which always glows."*

At that moment, the winds began to blow softly and then the calm, serene voice of Mother Nature came over them and said, "*I know why you have called on me. The child you ask about once used to be a Tooth Fairy just like all of you, and I named her Heart. Her job in the kingdom was to create laughter. When Heart would bring the baby teeth into the garden, she would share with me how at times she'd leave the kingdom and visit the children's homes. She would appear in her invisible form and spend most of the day with them. At times she would follow them to school or spend the evening in their homes. Heart would share with me all that she had seen. She would explain to me that because she was a Tooth Fairy, she knew she was not allowed to play with the children or talk with them. It was then she would ask me if she could become a child herself, but I would deny her request.*"

"*Then one day, Heart called on me again and reminded me that she had one wish as a Tooth Fairy. Pleading with me, she said, 'Please, Mother Nature, I wish to become a little girl. I know that I'm allowed only one wish in my eternal life, and that is what I really want.' So, I granted Heart her wish, with the agreement that she must return to us in seven years or she would remain a mortal forever. Heart agreed.*"

"*Now her time as a child is coming to an end,*" Mother Nature continued. "*As you can see, there are only six stars encircling your quarter moon.*"

All of the Tooth Fairies looked up at their moon. "*Each star represents one of you. When Heart left our kingdom, her star around your moon disappeared. When she returns to us, her star will reappear. This explains why Queen Melody was born with a crown of seven stars. In a very short time, I will give you a sign in the sky. On that night, your moon will become full and a moonbeam will lead you to*

Heart's room on Earth. It will be the only chance she will have to come home. This night will complete her seventh birthday. Queen Melody, I have chosen you to bring Heart home. You must appear in her dreams and remind her who she is."

"On the night your moon is full, you must go to Heart and sprinkle stardust on her. The stardust will turn her back into a Tooth Fairy. Then you will take her by the hand, step into the moonbeam and come home."

"Mother Nature," asked Queen Melody, "why did Heart want to be a child so badly? Was she not happy here?"

"It's not that she was unhappy," replied Mother Nature. *"She just thought she would love to be in their world. There she could have a mother and a father. She could go to school and have many friends. She was also intrigued by all the different children she had seen. Once she told me that if she had a chance to be a little girl she would have a friend of every kind. However, what she did not realize was that she would also experience feelings she had not known, like pain and sickness."*

"Why didn't you warn her?" asked Queen Melody.

Mother Nature then replied, *"She would still have wanted to go and find out for herself."*

All of the Tooth Fairies nodded their heads in understanding.

Suddenly, a white twinkling like stardust came over the garden. Mother Nature and the Tooth Fairies could see Heart's new life through the stardust.

Heart's name on Earth was Lisa.

~ Chapter Four ~

Heart's New Life

Heart lived on a dairy farm with parents who truly loved her. They knew they were as lucky to have her as she was to have them, for they had waited a long time to have a child. So, when Lisa arrived, they were just as happy as they could be.

Lisa loved her mother and father very much. There was no one as kind and as caring as they were. For instance, ever since Lisa could remember, her mother was able to charm everyone. She hoped to grow up to be just like her, loving and caring. Her mother's energies were endless, as she was always willing to endure whatever sacrifice it took to keep her family and friends happy.

There were times when Lisa would forget it was her turn to take cookies to school, even when her teacher reminded her and sent her home with a note. Lisa would still forget to give her mother the note; and the night before, she'd remember and hesitantly tell her mother. Her mother would then sigh in disbelief and still find a way to get those cookies to school on time.

As far back as Lisa could remember, the first thing she would hear in the morning when she woke up was her mother singing a song just for her. Then her mom would tickle her ribs and toes and sing in her ear until Lisa would wake up. She'd hug Lisa, give her a kiss and say, 'Good morning, Honey.'

When Lisa wasn't feeling well, her mother would fix her favorite breakfast which was hot cereal with ice cream or strawberries.

Sometimes she would make up a special occasion and take Lisa out for lunch, and just for fun, they'd start their lunch with dessert.

There were times when Lisa would sneak cookies out of the kitchen, and her mother would pretend she hadn't seen her. She'd merely say, 'Dinner will be ready soon.'

One of the kindest things Lisa remembered her mother doing was when Lisa needed a Little Red Riding Hood costume. As Lisa's mother was putting it together, halfway through, the sewing machine broke. Lisa's mother sat up all night on the eve of Halloween and finished the costume by hand. Lisa woke up the next morning and found her mother sleeping on the couch, with the costume on her lap. Lisa sang to her mother, tickled her ribs and toes to wake her up.

Lisa's father was a calm and patient man. Regardless of how busy he might be, he would try very hard to make time for Lisa. In the evenings before bedtime, Lisa would so many times climb up on her father's lap and say, 'Daddy, please read me a story,' and he always did.

Other times, they'd sit together on the front porch swing and he'd patiently listen to Lisa talk endlessly about school and her friends. On Sunday mornings, he'd take them to church, and then out for breakfast. Later in the evening, after dinner, he'd take them out for ice cream.

So, indeed, her life was good. However, there was something about Lisa that made her different in her new world. When Lisa was three years old, she fell out of a tree while playing and hurt her back badly and she was never able to walk properly again. As she got older, her left leg did not grow as long as her right leg. By the time she was five, one leg was visibly shorter than the other.

When Lisa started school, she was very excited. She loved a new adventure. However, once she was there, she was disappointed to find that not all children were kind. Some of the children picked on her and teased her because she walked with a limp. Lisa simply ignored them. It was difficult for her to understand why anyone would be so cruel. If she could change the way she walked, she would. It wasn't fun being teased. It would make her sad, but it would last only for a moment. For Lisa, there was always something to be happy about.

Lisa's happiness glowed in her face as well as her heart. She was always cheerful and her smile would light up the room. She could make anyone laugh and she made friends easily with people and animals.

In school, she had several friends, who were all different in their own special ways. What Lisa loved about them was that they were kind to her. To them it didn't matter that she limped when she walked. Her friends liked her just the way she was.

Lisa met her first school friend on the bus. After riding the bus for a few days, one little girl sat next to her and said, "You always have a smile on your face."

"Well," Lisa replied, "I like being happy, don't you?"

"Yes," said the little girl as she smiled back.

"What's your name?" asked Lisa.

"My name is Robbie. What's yours?"

"Lisa," she said with a smile. "If you want, I'll save a seat on the bus for you, so we can sit together every day, okay?"

"Okay," agreed Robbie. "You promise?"

"I promise," assured Lisa.

They sat together on the bus every day after that and became friends.

One day, while riding the bus, Robbie started singing in words that Lisa did not understand. Lisa was intrigued and quietly listened. After her friend was through, Lisa asked, "What were you singing? I didn't understand your song."

"That's because I'm singing in Spanish," replied Robbie. "I am Spanish, and I can speak both English and Spanish. I can sing songs that are in Spanish. I can teach you some words in Spanish, if you like, and maybe some Spanish songs, too!"

Lisa happily agreed. She quickly learned to say "*Hola*," which means, "Hello," and "*Como esta usted?*" which means, "How are you?" But Lisa's favorite phrase was "*Te Amo*" which means, "I love you."

On the bus, Lisa and her new friend giggled a lot, especially when Lisa tried so hard to roll her tongue for some of the new Spanish words she was learning. Lisa soon learned that Robbie would get teased because her family was poor. You could tell by the clothes she wore to school. They couldn't even afford a coat for Robbie. So, with her mom's permission, Lisa gave her one of her coats.

Lisa made another friend whose name was Katie. They were in the same class. Katie had curly blond hair and blue eyes, and she could tap dance. Lisa saw her tap dance during show-and-tell at school. Katie could see how Lisa was amazed by her talent and asked Lisa if she'd like to learn to tap dance. Lisa said, "No, thank you. I can't because I have one leg shorter than the other and dancing like that would hurt my back. But thank you for asking."

So, on days when Katie had dancing lessons after school, she would let Lisa wear her dancing shoes at recess. This way Lisa could see what her feet looked like in tap dancing shoes. Lisa would sit on the bench and move her feet, pretending to tap dance. Lisa really loved Katie for letting her do that. This friend, Katie, would get teased for having curly hair.

Lisa made another friend. Her name was Amber. They sat next to each other in class and Lisa noticed how Amber's eyes were shaped differently and what pretty straight black hair she had. But one day, Amber was wearing her hair up, and in her hair were two pretty chopsticks. So, in the cafeteria at lunch, Lisa went up to Amber and said, "May I sit with you and eat lunch?"

"Yes," replied Amber.

Lisa knew that by sitting closer to Amber, she could get a better look at those very pretty sticks she had in her hair.

"Why do you wear those sticks in your hair?" asked Lisa.

"Because I'm Japanese," Amber replied. "Where I come from we wear pretty things in our hair. They keep my hair from getting messy."

"They sure are pretty," said Lisa. "How can I get some?"

Amber immediately liked Lisa and said, "I'll ask my mom if we can get you some." So, Lisa and Amber also became very good friends. Lisa noticed that Amber would get teased because her eyes were different.

During recess, Lisa walked over to the playground to watch the children jump rope. One of the children asked Lisa to stand in line if she wanted to take a turn. Lisa noticed that some of the other children started laughing at her because she limped, but she knew not to pay attention to them—they were just being cruel.

"I was just watching." Lisa didn't explain that she couldn't jump; she simply walked away.

"I'll do your turn if you stay," a little girl named Marisa called out as Lisa walked away. So, Lisa decided to stay and let Marisa take her turn.

When they were done playing jump rope, Lisa thanked Marisa for her kindness.

"I enjoyed taking your turn playing jump rope," said Marisa. "I heard some other children laughing and making fun of you and I didn't want your feelings to be hurt. They're just bullies."

"Marisa," said Lisa, "they don't hurt my feelings. I know that they don't know any better. No one probably ever taught them that it isn't very nice to tease and make fun of people. My mom always says, 'Teach love, not hate.'"

Marisa really admired Lisa's courage. She knew just how cruel some children could be, because from time to time they would make fun of her because her skin was so dark. This little friend was African American. She was also teased badly for being heavy; she was heavier than most children her age.

Whenever the other children played jump rope, hopscotch, or any other game that required a lot of moving or jumping, Marisa would always stand in for Lisa and take her turn. That way Lisa wouldn't feel left out. Lisa loved having friends from all different cultures.

Not all of Lisa's friends were from school; she had one special little friend named Moses, who was a Native American.

Before Lisa had started school, Mose's mom, Judy, would babysit Lisa. Moses had not yet been born and Judy had become Lisa's second mom. And now, Judy was going to have a baby of her own.

One day, while Judy was babysitting Lisa and watching her play, Lisa took Judy by surprise and said, "Judy, your tummy's getting bigger."

Judy laughed and said, "You're right, sweetheart. I'm going to have a bady."

"There's a baby in your tummy? No, sir!" Lisa replied.

By that time, Judy realized that she was going to have to prove to Lisa that she really was carrying a baby in her tummy.

"Lisa, would you like to see the baby move? He's asleep right now, but if you want, we can wake him up?"

Lisa happily agreed.

So Judy gently pushed one side of her stomach, then the other side. She kept doing that until right before Lisa's eyes, Judy's stomach started to move. Lisa watched in amazement, thinking to herself, "Oh, my goodness, there really is a baby in there!"

Judy was carefully watching Lisa to see how she would react.

Judy looked at Lisa and asked, "Now, do you believe me? There really is a baby in there?"

"Yes," replied Lisa. Then, with a very concerned look on her face, she asked, "Judy, did you eat your baby?"

Judy laughed out loud and replied, "Of course not, silly, that's just where babies live until it's time for them to be born."

After that day, Lisa became even closer to Judy. Lisa felt she was sharing something very special with her. From time to time, Lisa would ask Judy if the baby was moving. At times he was and Lisa would watch in delight. Sometimes, they would sit together and talk about Baby Moses and wonder what he would be like.

"How do you know it's a boy?" asked Lisa.

"Because, Lisa," Judy replied, giving Lisa a sincere look, "it's what I want with all my heart. When you want something with all your heart, it means you want it very badly and you will usually get it. All of your wishes and dreams won't come true unless you really believe. My heart tells me that it's a boy, and I went to the doctor and he said it was a boy, too."

The big day finally came. The baby was born, and he was a boy just as Judy had said.

From the first moment Lisa saw Moses and held him in her arms, she said, "I'm going to call you Moe and we're going to be the best of buddies."

Heart

~ Chapter Five ~

The Dream

Mother Nature removed all the white twinkling star dust from the air that she used to tell the story about Heart. The air now was clear, and the Tooth Fairies could see each other once again.

The Tooth Fairies had now seen all of Heart's family and friends and were very pleased with her life on Earth. However, Mother Nature had not yet shared all that she knew about Heart's life.

"Mother Nature, why did we not miss Heart?" asked Garnet.

As the winds faintly blew and the flowers swayed in the breeze, Mother Nature replied, *"Because I did not give you memory of her. I also did not give you the feelings of sickness, pain, sorrow, envy, jealousy, fear or greed. Those feelings come from an evil force, which inflicted injury and pain upon Heart—and very soon, Heart will no longer be able to walk. Her back problem will become much worse and soon you will see her in a wheelchair. Queen Melody, it's almost time for Heart to come home. You must reach Heart through her dreams and remind her of her life here as a Tooth Fairy. Remember, to look into the night sky for the full moon, for this will be your only chance to bring Heart home."* Then the winds stopped and Mother Nature's voice disappeared.

At first Queen Melody was very quiet and didn't know how to react to what she just had heard. The other Tooth Fairies could see that she was in deep thought. They knew exactly what she was thinking. She really had been given something special to do.

Queen Melody excused herself and flew off to the castle and into her room. She sat on her bed, crossed her legs, buried her hands under her chin and started to think. Queen Melody decided to approach Lisa in her dreams that very night. Later, she would tell the rest of the Tooth Fairies about her plans to visit Heart. But for now, she was tired and laid down to rest.

Later that day, when Queen Melody awoke from her nap, she flew into the garden to talk with the Tooth Fairies. When they saw her, they instantly knew why she was there and gathered around her.

That evening, all of the Tooth Fairies waited patiently for Heart to fall asleep. As she slept, Queen Melody slipped into her dream and appeared to Heart in a glowing light, and spoke to Heart without moving her lips.

"Lisa, you are a Tooth Fairy. It will soon be time for you to come home." Then Queen Melody disappeared.

Lisa woke up early the next morning. She remembered her dream, but she was confused because she didn't understand it. Lisa's mother was surprised to find her already up when she came in the room to wake Lisa up for school.

"Mother," cried Lisa, "I had a dream about a Tooth Fairy last night."

"Oh," said Lisa's mother, "what did she look like?"

"She was so beautiful and she glowed all over. She stood there and just stared at me. I know she was trying to tell me something, but I couldn't understand what she was saying. She wasn't moving her lips, but I know she was trying to tell me something. Gosh, Mother, she was so beautiful! She was so real."

"Well," said her mother, "It must have been a wonderful dream, but you need to start getting ready or you'll be late for school."

"Mother, I just know she was trying to tell me something," Lisa exclaimed as her mother turned to leave the room.

~ Chapter Six ~

The Magical Wings

Queen Melody woke up the next morning, sat up in bed; and in her heart, she knew Lisa had not understood her. Then, she thought about Garnet and knew they had to talk.

At that precise moment, Garnet appeared in Queen Melody's room. Queen Melody giggled when she saw Garnet standing there.

"You wanted to speak to me?" asked Garnet.

"Yes," replied Queen Melody, "I had another dream about Heart last night, only this time I went into her dream and spoke to her like we planned. I tried telling her that she was a Tooth Fairy and that it was time for her to come home, but I don't think she understood me."

"Don't worry," said Garnet. "She will remember later when she least expects it. Just wait and you'll see. Now, if you'll please get out of bed, we can go play in the garden."

Into the garden they flew, carrying themselves several inches off the ground, fluttering their wings ever so gently and swaying to the music the winds had created.

All of the Tooth Fairies loved to play in the garden. It was such a wonderful place to be. Everything there glowed brilliantly. There were small rainbows to water the garden, which the Tooth Fairies used as slides. There were also fish in the lake for the Tooth Fairies to play with. The mushrooms always changed colors and the willow trees would sway in the wind. As the Tooth Fairies heard the music, they would hum along, and the butterflies and mushrooms would join in, too. The fish would take turns jumping out of the water to dance on the lake's surface. They loved to entertain the Tooth Fairies. The flowers would put out more fragrance; the smaller rainbows would take turns glowing to the beat of the music; and the air sparkled with stardust.

When the music died down, the Tooth Fairies decided to play their favorite game of Hide-and-Seek. They could disappear which made the game much more fun.

All of a sudden, Garnet had the urge to chase and tickle Queen Melody, so off she flew. Queen Melody saw Garnet flying towards her and knew by the look on Garnet's face that she wanted to tickle her. Queen Melody flew as fast as she could through the garden trying to escape from Garnet. As she tried to get away, one of her wings caught on a branch and was slashed. Suddenly, Queen Melody fell to the ground.

All the other Tooth Fairies sensed something was wrong and immediately flew to her side.

"I've torn my wing," sighed Queen Melody. "Now I won't be able to play anymore." Then she thought of something even worse. How would she get Heart back to the kingdom without her powers? Now she was very worried. Mother Nature had warned her that if she injured her wings in any way, she would lose her powers until they mended.

The Tooth Fairies knew what she was thinking. They gathered around her, lifted Queen Melody and flew her back to the Crystal Castle and into her room. They set her gently on her bed. They were very careful not to tear her wing any further. Queen Melody fell asleep. That night, she again dreamed of Heart, but now she was powerless to reach her. She could only watch her sleep.

The next morning, Queen Melody woke up with Heart on her mind. This time she was unable to mentally make contact, no matter how hard she tried, forgetting she had lost her powers. Queen Melody sat on her bed patiently waiting for someone to check in on her. She didn't move. She worried that if she tried to move on her own, she might tear her fragile wing again.

Suddenly, the Tooth Fairies appeared one by one, standing around her bed, wanting to know if she was all right. They gently helped her sit up.

"Queen Melody, would you like something to eat? I've brought you some fruit," said Eden, offering her a pomegranate and a banana.

"Thank you," replied Queen Melody. "You've brought my favorite foods."

"We also brought you something to drink," said Eden, as she presented a pomegranate shell brimming with water.

Queen Melody looked at all the Tooth Fairies and said, "Somehow, I feel that all of you must know by now what I'm thinking."

"Surely, your Majesty, you know that we would be happy to help you with Heart if we could," said Crystal. "We know that you are no longer able to use your powers to reach her."

"Don't worry," said Dusk. "We've already discussed it among ourselves, and with your permission, we have a plan."

"What kind of plan?" asked Queen Melody.

"Well," replied Dusk, as she anxiously went on to explain, "Crystal is going to reach Heart and help her understand what you were trying to tell her the night you appeared in her dream. While

Heart is sleeping, Crystal will bring her back into the kingdom. Maybe when Heart sees the kingdom again, she'll remember who she really is and she'll want to come back."

"That's a wonderful idea," said Queen Melody. "Thank you so much. Now I must sleep and allow my wings to mend."

Rainbow

~ Chapter Seven ~

A Slumber Party

It was Friday night. Lisa had invited all her new school friends to spend the weekend with her at the dairy farm.

Lisa's mother baked cookies for them and the girls knew that whenever they went to Lisa's house, they could eat as many cookies and drink as much milk as they wanted. They could stay up late and laugh and talk about anything they wanted to.

On Saturday morning, they got up and got dressed, giggled a lot and talked some more. Then, they headed down to the barn with Lisa's father for they always enjoyed helping him feed the cows and the calves.

In the meantime, Lisa's mother stayed behind and prepared breakfast, because she knew they'd be hungry when they returned.

After breakfast, they went outside and played in the yard. Once in a while a butterfly would come by and actually land on Lisa. Butterflies seemed to be attracted to her. There were times her friends actually had seen Lisa walk over to a butterfly, slip her hand underneath it, and walk around with it on her hand.

Then the girls decided to play Hide-and-Seek.

"Come on, Lisa," said Amber. "You're it."

"No," replied Lisa, "I'd rather just lay here on the grass and rest. I'm feeling a little tired."

"Okay," replied Amber as she cheerfully skipped away, "we'll play later."

Lisa sat on the grass. Then, she decided to lie on her back, placing her hands behind her head and crossing one leg on top of the other. She was simply enjoying the sun, when suddenly—out of nowhere—a huge rainbow formed above her head and a soft, gentle voice came to her.

"Lisa, this is the answer to the dream you didn't understand," the soft, gentle voice instructed. "You are a Tooth Fairy and it's time for you to come home. I will bring you back to the kingdom while you sleep and you'll then remember who you are."

Then, her friend Amber came back and gently tapped her on the head.

"Lisa, come out, come out, wherever you are! What are you doing—daydreaming?"

Lisa looked up at Amber and smiled, "Yep, I sure was."

Lisa did not want to talk about what had just happened because she felt Amber would not understand and might not believe her.

Later that day, after all of her friends had gone home, Lisa went back to her room to think about what had happened to her. Was it real? In her heart she knew it was, but who could she share it with? Who would believe her? Then she thought of her little friend Moe.

Moe had been her friend before he'd been born. Yes, she could tell Moe. They understood each other very well.

"I'll call him up right now," she thought. "No...I'll wait until he comes over."

That evening, after her friends left, Lisa's tooth fell out. She excitedly showed it to her mother, and then went to her room and placed it under her pillow. Before going to sleep, she knelt beside her bed, put her hands together and prayed that the Tooth Fairy would come to her house. While Lisa slept, Crystal appeared and gently slipped her hand under Lisa's pillow, taking the tooth and replacing it with a ***Golden Coin***.

The Gold Coin

~ Chapter Eight ~

The Secret

Several weeks had gone by and Lisa still had not seen Moe.

Now the pain in her back had become so bad she could no longer walk or go to school. This made her very sad, because she loved school and missed seeing her friends every day.

Lisa was now in a wheelchair, but to her that was not as bad as not being able to go to school; and most importantly, her tooth had finally fallen out and she had no one to share it with.

Lisa was out of school for a whole month. Her parents searched for a teacher or tutor who could help Lisa learn her lessons at home. Within a few days, they found a great teacher. Her name was Mrs. Conner. Mrs. Conner was pretty and nice. Every week she brought Lisa a treat. Lisa knew she was lucky to have her very own teacher, but she still missed her friends. However, she did have a friend she could see whenever she wanted. It was her little friend, Moe.

Lisa had an unusual ability to think about someone and that person would soon call her or pay her a visit.

On this particular day, it was her friend Moe whom she wanted to see. She couldn't stop thinking about him. That afternoon, after Mrs. Conner left, Lisa and her mother were in the kitchen having a snack when the phone rang. Lo and behold, it was Moe's mom, Judy.

She was calling to see if they could come over for a brief visit. Lisa overheard the conversation.

"Hi, Judy. What's up?" said Lisa's mother. Then, after a pause, "Sure. Come on over." She then hung up the phone.

"Moe and Judy are coming over," Lisa's mother said to her. "They're going to bring us some cheesecake."

Twenty minutes later, the doorbell rang. It was Moe and Judy. As Lisa's mother opened the door, Moe was already trying to push his way past Judy and the cheesecake. As soon as Moe and his mother entered the room, they saw Lisa in her wheelchair. They were both very surprised. It had been over a month since they'd last seen Lisa.

"Honey, when did you get the wheelchair and why do you need it?" Judy asked as she walked over to Lisa.

"Well, it's my legs," replied Lisa. "I'm not able to move them very well anymore."

Lisa's mother could see that it was making Lisa uncomfortable to talk about it, so she politely interrupted and asked Lisa to take Moe to her room to play. She'd call them later to have some cheesecake.

Lisa wheeled herself towards her bedroom.

Moe asked, "Can I have a ride?"

"Sure," Lisa quickly answered. "See those small bars on the back in the middle? Stand on those very gently."

Moe put his feet on the small bars and then Lisa pushed the control button and they wheeled themselves into her room.

As Judy and Lisa's mother walked into the kitchen, Judy asked, "Is Lisa's wheelchair permanent?"

"Maybe," Lisa's mother replied. "The doctor said it might be."

"Oh, I'm sorry. Is there anything I can do for you or Lisa?" asked Judy, very sincerely.

"Yes, there is. You can cut her a piece of your delicious cheese-cake."

When Lisa and Moe were in the bedroom, Moe jumped off the wheelchair, and noticed that Lisa was not getting up. Since he'd never seen a wheelchair before, he said, "Lisa, if you want to play, you've got to get out of that chair."

The remark almost made Lisa laugh, but instead all she said was, "Moe, I don't feel well and I have to stay sitting down. But I can still play games! Later, I'll get my mother to take some down from the closet. Right now I want to tell you a secret."

"Moe, do you know what a secret is?"

"No," Moe said, shaking his head.

"Well, a secret is when you tell someone something you don't want anyone else to know. It's like a game. A secret is something you can't tell anyone else or it won't be a secret anymore. So Moe, do you want to know a secret?"

Moe was so in awe over this new game that all he could do was nod.

"Well, you have to promise me with all your heart that you won't tell anybody else our secret."

Moe happily agreed.

"Moe, I had a dream," Lisa said in a low voice, "that I was a Tooth Fairy."

"What's a Tooth Fairy?" Moe asked in surprise.

Lisa wheeled herself over to her dresser, opened the drawer and pulled out a beautiful, sparkling gold coin. She opened her mouth and pointed to the empty space. "See this. It is where my baby tooth fell out! Moe, there comes a time when you lose your baby teeth, and if you put them under your pillow, a Tooth Fairy comes and takes them during the night, and then leaves you money."

Moe was very surprised and said, "And you get money?"

"Yes," said Lisa happily, as she held up the gold coin. "This is what I got, a gold coin!"

"Will I lose my teeth?" asked Moe.

"Yes, and you'll get money when you lose your baby teeth, but you must put the tooth under your pillow."

"When will I lose my first tooth?"

"I think when you are six or seven like me or a little sooner—maybe when you're eight. I'm not really sure. My mother says it's different for everyone. Now, let me tell you about my dream. Remember, it's a secret, okay?"

"Okay," replied Moe.

"Moe," Lisa said, "I had a dream that I went to a place that had a castle made of glass, and it sat right on top of the clouds. It was beautiful! The castle had a big hallway going right through the middle of it. In the castle, you could see butterflies flying all around. There were clouds around the castle like a wall. I walked on the castle sidewalk made of clouds and was able to walk right through the walls. There were rooms with beds and pillows and the floors were made of flowers. In each room was a star floating in the air like magic. As I walked through, I noticed that my feet did not touch the floor. There were seven rooms and two of the rooms were different. One room glowed brightly and the other had a gold circle of light around the bed. As I went through the hallway and reached the outside, I saw the most beautiful garden I'd ever seen."

"There were walking, talking mushrooms and the sound of music everywhere. The mushrooms and the butterflies could change colors," Lisa continued. "There was lots of green grass and trees. All the flowers had pretty smiling faces on them and everything glowed. In this garden, there was a clear blue lake that sparkled. As I moved closer to the lake, beautiful little fairies appeared."

"What's a fairy?" asked Moe.

"They look like people, but they're very small and have wings like a butterfly. As the fairies came towards me, I noticed I was the same size they were. When I looked into the lake I saw twinkling stars. It was so clear that you could see all the way to the bottom. As I looked closely into the water, I saw myself. My hair was long and blond, and my face looked perfect and beautiful much like a doll's. The clothes I was wearing were different. I wore a beautiful red dress that twinkled and a glowing red star floated above my head. The fairies and I were all dressed alike, except that we were all wearing different colors."

"When I looked down into the lake, I could see brightly colored fish. The fish would go down to the bottom of the lake and pick up shells with their mouths. Then, they would swim back up. As soon as they reached the surface, the shells would turn into coins. A Tooth Fairy sitting on a floating flower took the money and disappeared. I saw a fish dancing on the water moving about on its tail. As I stood watching, I remembered wishing with all my heart that I could stay there forever."

"When I looked across the lake," Lisa continued, "I saw fairies using little rainbows as slides, while others would disappear and reappear as though they were playing Hide-and-Seek."

"There was one Tooth Fairy who stood by the lake watching me—she was the same Tooth Fairy I dreamt about. In the dream, I felt she was talking to me but she didn't move her lips. One day while I was lying on the grass, a rainbow formed above my head and a voice said to me, 'You are a Tooth Fairy and it's time for you to come home.'"

"Moe, maybe they're coming for me. I hope so! I know that when you want something very badly, you have to want it with all your heart to get it. You know who told me that?"

Moe shook his head, no.

"Your mom. Moe, do you know what this means?" Lisa asked.

Again, Moe shook his head, no.

"It means I'm going home, my real home. My real home is a castle. I won't be in pain anymore. Looking surprised, Lisa said,

"Maybe that is why I was given a gold coin! Even my mom was surprised that I got a gold coin."

"I want to go there with you," Moe said, looking sad.

"Oh, Moe," replied Lisa, "I wish you could. But it seems that only Fairies are allowed to live there."

"Please, can I go with you?" Moe asked again, begging.

Lisa put his little hands in hers and said, "Maybe I'll be back when you lose a tooth."

Then Lisa heard someone coming towards her room.

"Moe! Someone's coming! Remember, this is a secret," she reminded him. The door opened and it was Moe's mom.

Moe quickly ran over to Lisa and with tears in his eyes, gave her the biggest hug he had ever given her. His mom looked at him with concern.

"My goodness! What seems to be going on here?" asked Judy. "I came to bring you guys a piece of cheesecake. What is all of this?"

Moe looked at his mom with tears in his eyes and said, "I'm not hungry."

"Well," said Judy, "It's time to leave anyway." She picked Moe up in her arms.

"Honey, we will be back soon to visit," she said to Lisa. She then bent over and gave Lisa a hug.

As they were leaving, Lisa called to Moe and said, "Next time you come over, we'll play some of those games I told you about." She then winked at him and blew him a kiss goodbye.

Later that afternoon, Lisa sat on her bed, thinking about how she really would miss Moe and all the happy times they'd spent together. After all, they'd been best friends since before he was born. It was hard for her to imagine that she might never see him again. Her biggest concern now was that she might be leaving her family and friends behind.

The Crystal Castle

~ Chapter Nine ~

The Seventh Star

A few weeks had passed. The Tooth Fairies were constantly watching Queen Melody's every move, checking her wings, always asking, 'Are they healing? How do you feel? Can you fly yet?'

Queen Melody would try and try with all her heart to lift herself from her bed and nothing!

The fairies were constantly saying to one another, "Time is running out. We're not going to reach Heart in time."

Another fairy would say, "Oh, yes, we will. I know we will. We know Mother Nature is in control."

"Yes. Yes," they'd say to each other.

Queen Melody would watch them floating around, always thinking of what they could do to help. She'd giggle and say, "Quit it, you're making me tired. Stop it. Go play." The Fairies would giggle and off they'd fly.

At last, Queen Melody woke up one morning and decided that her wings felt strong enough to try her powers again. She started by lifting herself slowly off the bed. Then down she went. She said to herself, 'I can do this,' and tried again and nothing! Once again, up she went, and down again she came. On her third try, she sat and concentrated with all her heart and all her might. She started lifting herself up, flapping her wings forward and backward; and all of a sudden, up she went—higher and higher until she knew she had finally succeeded. She was so happy and flew carefully into the garden. There she waited for the other Tooth Fairies to join her. She flew over to the flowers and smelled them. Next, she flew over to a floating flower, sat on it, and floated about the lake happily humming and singing. She was so happy to be up and about. The flowers, the trees, and the winds joined her in song. The fish swam about her, jumping out of the water in joy. It was their way of letting Queen Melody know they had missed her. The fish managed to put a huge smile on her face, and her smile was indeed beautiful. For when she smiled, her face became even brighter. The willow trees began to clap and the mushrooms glowed off and on. Everyone was delighted.

Suddenly all of the Tooth Fairies were standing on the edge of the lake, smiling and hugging each other. They were excited to see that Queen Melody's powers were restored.

They all hopped on the floating flowers and moved across the lake's surface to join their Queen. When they reached her, the floating flowers took flight and circled around Queen Melody, surrounding her with love and energy. They played until dusk. Then the music that Queen Melody had created slowly came to a stop. The floating flowers brought the Tooth Fairies back down to the water's surface, and Queen Melody began to speak.

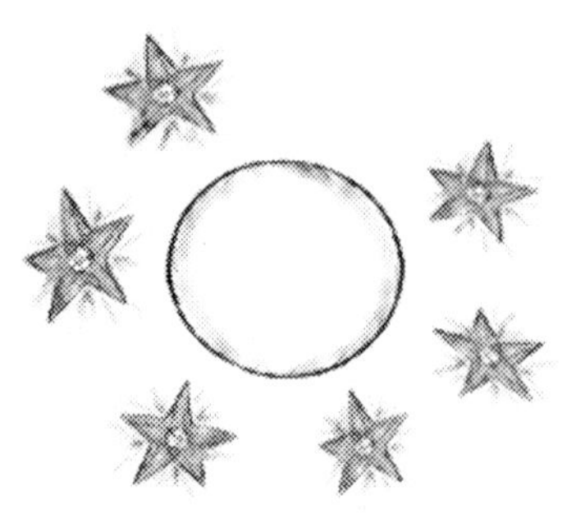

"Look! Look to the sky! Our moon is full! Hurry! We must tend to Heart quickly! We must make our plans now for her seven years are at an end."

With that in mind, they all flew back to the shore and settled onto the grass. Once again, they joined hands and formed a circle around Queen Melody. As they danced around her, they all started to glow with energy. The Tooth Fairies could actually hear Queen Melody thinking out loud.

"Crystal has already prepared Heart's room. Mother Nature is providing us with the moonbeam. Heart will be sleeping soon. Everything is falling into place tonight."

Queen Melody flew to Heart's room and saw that stardust had been sprinkled on her bed and butterflies had been brought in for decoration. Fresh flower pedals had been placed on her bed. The gold circle of light appeared more brilliant than ever. The butterflies appeared to be dancing. A brilliant star floated gracefully through the air. Everything was now in its proper place for Heart's Homecoming.

The Tooth Fairy Dusk flew out to the center of the garden, bowed, and said, "Good night, Evening Sky." And she quickly flew back into the castle where the rest of the Tooth Fairies were waiting for Heart's return.

When all was completed, they flew back into the garden and waited with Queen Melody until Heart fell asleep. When they knew she had finally fallen into a deep sleep, they joined hands and came together in a small circle which gave them the glowing energy.

The spirit of Mother Nature appeared in their minds rather than by sight, and spoke to them saying:

"The moonbeam I promised is granted."

It instantly appeared before them and lit up the entire kingdom. Thousands of sparkling stars filled the moonbeam. There was magic in the air. A wand filled with magical stardust appeared in Queen Melody's hand. With that, Queen Melody stepped into the moonbeam and vanished. She reappeared in Heart's room on Earth.

Queen Melody effortlessly flew over to Heart's bed, lifted her wand and sprinkled stardust over her. She leaned forward and placed the wand on Heart's forehead; then Heart opened her eyes and instantly remembered who she was. She smiled and reached out to touch Queen Melody's hand. Immediately, her blond hair began to grow and her body became smaller, until she was only twelve inches tall. Her clothes became those of a Tooth Fairy, and her color was red. Her eyes began to twinkle; then her wings appeared and she began to glow. Now Lisa was no longer Lisa. She was once again the Tooth Fairy, Heart.

"Are you ready to go home now?" asked Queen Melody, as Heart stood up, fluttering her wings. "Do you know who you are?"

"Yes, but who are you? You look like a Tooth Fairy, but I don't know you. I've never seen you before."

"I am your Queen. I arrived after you left the kingdom." Queen Melody went on to explain to her what had happened while she had been away. Then once again she asked, "Are you ready to come home?"

"Yes," answered Heart.

As they started towards the moonbeam, Heart suddenly stopped.

"Please wait," she said. "I can't just leave here and leave the people who love me! What about my mother and father? What about all my friends? They'll miss me and wonder what happened to me."

"Oh, dear," exclaimed Queen Melody. "We didn't think about that!"

Neither Heart nor Queen Melody knew what to do. Queen Melody flew over and sat on the edge of the bed post with her legs crossed, placed her chin between her hands and began to think. It was her favorite thinking position. Heart flew over and stood next to her.

"I know," Queen Melody exclaimed excitedly. "Let's create a new Lisa!"

"Yes, but what about my little friend, Moe? I told him all about my dream. He will know I've become a Tooth Fairy again. What about him?" asked Heart.

"Well, you have the power to make him forget what you told him," explained Queen Melody.

So, Heart remembered how to use her powers and did just that. She went into deep thought and made Moe forget the story she'd told him. Then she looked back at what used to be her bed and stepped closer to the edge.

Queen Melody handed her wand to Heart and said, "Sprinkle star dust on the bed. You can create a new Lisa." So, Heart moved the wand back and forth, sprinkling star dust on the bed, and a new Lisa was created. Then, with one last wave of the wand, she said, "Lisa, you will walk again."

Heart then spoke to Lisa as she slept:

"Lisa, in your world there is fear, sickness, pain, greed, jealousy, and anger; but you, as a human on earth, have your own magical powers. You have the power of courage. You have the power to love or hate, to be good or bad, selfish or giving, rich or poor. However, the world will try to confuse you about what is right or wrong. You have the power to make the right decisions. You have the power to make all your dreams come true, and the greatest of all the powers you possess is love. It is important to use love; you must always remember that."

Then she stepped back, blowing life into Lisa and said,

"This child I recreate of me
Shall be a light for all to see."

Queen Melody flew off the bed post to the edge of Lisa's bed, looked at Heart and said, "We must hurry before the moonbeam disappears!"

Queen Melody took Heart by the hand. Together they flew into the moonbeam and off into the night.

Then something wonderful happened. The Tooth Fairies regained the seventh star around their moon. Heart was finally home.

~ The End ~

Heart's final message...

There really is magic in believing!
You are a ***miracle!***
Continue to ***dream!***
May all your ***wishes*** *come true!*

Glossary

Bully: Someone who picks on you

Dream: Something lovely, beautiful, wonderful, special—you can only see while you are sleeping

Fairy: A graceful imaginary being in human form with magical powers

Fairy tale: An enchanting, make-believe story with a happy ending

Homework: School work done at home

Love: Liking someone or something with all of your heart

Magic: Moving things without touching them; disappearing and reappearing; and things that can't be explained

Miracle: Things that happen that are hard to believe

Moderation: Not too much of anything (like not too much candy, because it's not good for you)

Secret: Something you don't want anyone else to know

Tell! Tell! Tell!... when something isn't right!

Have you ever held a butterfly more than once?

Have you ever had mushrooms grow out of the middle of your bedroom floor?

Have you ever been inside a rainbow?

Have you ever had a wish come true?

Have you ever heard the voice of God?

Margaret has a passion for things money can't buy. She believes in Faith, Hope, Love and Miracles. She believes that children are the most important people in the world, and good friends are the greatest gift of all. She knows that if you trust, obey, believe and do what's right; add a little dedication and never give up—you, too, can achieve all the desires of your heart and make any dream come true.

About the Author "Margaret"

God Bless America!

Margaret was an Ambassador Guide for the United States Olympic Committee from 1994 to 2005. Currently, she is a member of the Manitou Springs Historical Society in Manitou Springs, Colorado; she also serves as a volunteer at the Miramont Castle in Manitou Springs.

Margaret's ultimate passion is to help children in need. She lives in Colorado Springs, Colorado with her family and believes in living happily ever after…

The Seven Magical Tooth Fairies
Brush Your Teeth * Do Not Talk To Strangers * Don't Be A Bully * Eat Candy In Moderation * Do Your Homework *
Heart
Imagery... Images of the mind manifested.

The Seven Magical Teeth Fairies
Do Your Homework * Brush Your Teeth * Do Not Talk To Strangers *
Eat Candy In Moderation * Don't Be A Bully
Imagery... Images of the mind manifested.
The Gold Coin

If you would like to share your thoughts with Margaret about the book, send letters to:

P.O. Box 6926
Colorado Springs, CO 80934

Margaret can be reached at the Miramont Castle (719) 685-1011

Books may be purchased at Amazon.com, Borders.com, BarnesandNoble.com, booksamillion.com, & iUniverse.com

Coming soon!
www.thesevenmagicaltoothfairies.com

Wish for Peace!

iUniverse.com

978-0-595-37420-5
0-595-37420-4

CPSIA information can be obtained at www.ICGtesting.com
Printed in the USA
BVOW031104190213

313663BV00001B/3/A